Getting Your Zzzzs

Sing Along — Tune: If You're Happy and You Know It

Jo Cleland

Rourke Educational Media

rourkeeducationalmedia.com

Teacher Notes available at
rem4teachers.com

www.rourkeeducationalmedia.com

PHOTO CREDITS: Cover: © Александр Васильев; Title page: © Csaba Toth; page 3: © ACKY YEUNG; page 4: © Jani Bryson; page 5: © drbimages; page 6: © clu; page 7, 12: © jianying yin; page 8: © GraÃ§a Victoria; page 9: © nicole waring; page 10: © Shawn Gearhart; page 11: © Ana Abejon; page 13: © Steve Debenport; page 14, 17, 19: © Chris Fertnig; page 15: © Damir Cudic; page 16: © Imgorthand; page 18: © Kim Gunkel; page 20: © Belinda Pretorius; page 21: © Benjamin Loo

Editor: Precious McKenzie

Cover Design by Tara Raymo
Page Design by Mikala Collins

Library of Congress EPCN Data

Getting Your Zzzzs / Jo Cleland
(Sing and Read, Healthy Habits, K-2)
ISBN 978-1-61810-085-6 (hard cover)(alk. paper)
ISBN 978-1-61810-218-8 (soft cover)
Library of Congress Control Number: 2011944395

Rourke Educational Media
Printed in the United States of America,
North Mankato, Minnesota

rourkeeducationalmedia.com

customerservice@rourkeeducationalmedia.com • PO Box 643328 Vero Beach, Florida 32964

If I don't sleep well
I'm not so **strong**.

If I don't sleep well
the day's so long.

5

If I don't sleep well,

if I don't sleep well,

if I don't sleep well things go wrong!

If I get my Zzzzs every night,

if I get my Zzzzs my **brain** is **bright**.

If I get my Zzzzs, if I get my Zzzzs,
if I get my Zzzzs things go right.

13

If I get my Zzzzs I fight **disease**.

I'm not so likely to **sneeze**.

If I get my Zzzzs, if I get my Zzzzs,

if I get my Zzzzs life's a **breeze**!

Glossary

brain (brayn): organ in your head that controls your body

breeze (breez): easy way to be

bright (BRITE): smart, alert

disease (duh-zeez): sickness

sneeze (SNEEZ): a reflex that blows air out of your nose when you have a cold

strong (strong): hard to break or powerful

Getting Your Zzzzs

Tune: If You're Happy and You Know It

If I don't sleep well I'm not so strong.
If I don't sleep well the day's so long.

If I don't sleep well, if I don't sleep well,
if I don't sleep well things go wrong!

If I get my Zzzzs every night,
if I get my Zzzzs my brain is bright.

If I get my Zzzzs, if I get my Zzzzs,
if I get my Zzzzs things go right.

If I get my Zzzzs I fight disease.
I'm not so likely to sneeze.

If I get my Zzzzs, if I get my Zzzzs,
if I get my Zzzzs life's a breeze!

Index

Websites

kidshealth.org/kid/stay_healthy/body/cant_sleep.html

www.sciencekids.co.nz/gamesactivities/healthgrowth.html

www.sleepforkids.org/html/head.html

About the Author

Jo Cleland enjoys writing books, composing songs, and making games. She loves to read, sing, and play games with children.

Ask The Author!
www.rem4students.com